DIANNE HOFMEYR grew up in Gordon's Bay, South Africa.
She graduated as an art teacher in Cape Town and has written five teenage novels.
The Sunday Telegraph, reviewing *The Stone*, her first book for Frances Lincoln,
commented that "both text and pictures glow with mystical allure."
Her most recent collaboration with Jude Daly is *The Faraway Island*.
Dianne lives in southwest London.

JUDE DALY's titles for Frances Lincoln include *The Gift of the Sun*,
written by Dianne Stewart and chosen as one of Child Education's Best Books of 1996;
The Stone and *The Faraway Island* by Dianne Hofmeyr;
The Elephant's Pillow, written by Diana Reynolds Roome;
Lila and the Secret of Rain by David Conway and *To Every Thing there is a Season*.
Jude lives in Cape Town with her husband, the writer and illustrator Niki Daly.

For my two young friends Faye and Marie, who live in Egypt – D.H.
For my brother Andrew – J.D.

The Star-Bearer copyright © Frances Lincoln Limited 2001
Text copyright © Dianne Hofmeyr 2001
Illustrations copyright © Jude Daly 2001
By arrangement with The Inkman, Cape Town, South Africa

Hand Lettering by Andrew van der Merwe

First published in Great Britain in 2001 by
Frances Lincoln Children's Books, 4 Torriano Mews,
Torriano Avenue, London NW5 2RZ
www.franceslincoln.com

This edition published 2008

British Library Cataloguing in Publication Data available on request

ISBN 978-1-84507-838-6

Set in Baker Signet

Printed in China

9 8 7 6 5 4 3 2 1

The STAR-BEARER

A Creation Myth from Ancient Egypt

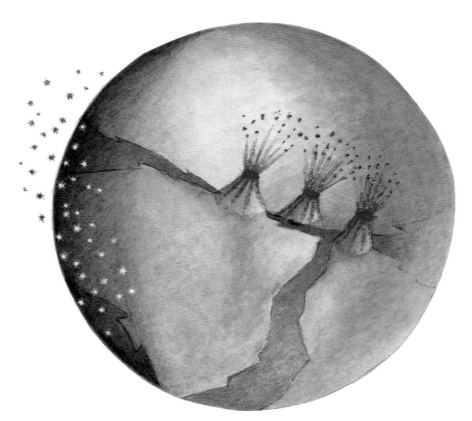

Dianne Hofmeyr • Jude Daly

F

FRANCES LINCOLN

CHILDREN'S BOOKS

Three distinct groups of ancient Egyptian myths stem from the cities of Heliopolis, Hermopolis and Memphis. Stories are often inconsistent even within one group. This story is based on the Heliopolis creation myth. Accounts of the myth can be found in the Pyramid Texts, the oldest literature in the world, dating from 3000 BC, which were preserved in the royal pyramids of the 5th and 6th Dynasties. The myth is also to be found in the later Coffin Texts and the Book of the Dead, dating from the 12th and 13th Dynasties.

HOW TO PRONOUNCE THE NAMES
Atum – AH-TUM
Shu – SHOO
Tefnut – TEF-NOOT
Geb – as in GET
Nut – NOOT

In the beginning, there was nothing but darkness and water that lay cold and still as black marble. Nothing moved in the inky silence.

After countless ages, a ripple formed beneath the black water and the bud of a lotus
flower pushed upwards. As the petals slowly unfurled, they spread a blue lustre
in the darkness. Enclosed in the centre of the bloom was the golden godchild, Atum.

Atum stood up and cast the first gleam of brilliant light into the world. But before he could take pleasure in the splendour, the flower pulled him back into its heart and sank into the dark depths again.

This happened again and again. Atum grew lonely with nothing but dark and light to keep him company. He longed for friends. So he blew across the surface of his hands in all directions: "Shu ... shu ... shu ..." Gusts of air swirled around him and then swept away across the watery waste – this was Shu, god of air.

Atum tried even harder. He blew over his hands again. "Tff ... tff ... tff ..."
Drops of moisture flew in all directions – this was Tefnut, goddess of dew and rain.

Shu and Tefnut loved to tease and play.

They raced about in wide circles, chasing each other over the surface of the water.

Shu blew up windstorms that drew the water into waves.

Tefnut threw down rain that beat it flat again.

Shu was blustery, and rasped and pounded. Tefnut was often tearful. She drizzled and drenched and spouted.

Together they were unrestrained, unpredictable and tempestuous.

Shu and Tefnut had two children. Their son Geb, god of the earth, grew up green as jade with all the rain his mother showered on him. And their daughter Nut, goddess of the sky, grew up pure as aquamarine with all the love her father wrapped around her.

Geb and Nut were quieter than their parents. They clasped one another and laughed and whispered secrets in each other's ears. Sky clung to earth and earth to sky. They were inseparable.

Atum the creator was upset. "I have work to do. I need space for my creation. If you stay so close to one another, there will be no room for tall trees and rugged mountains, for rivers and waterfalls and creatures with tall legs and long necks!"

But Geb and Nut took no notice. They went on laughing and whispering secrets to one another.

Eventually Atum grew impatient and summoned Shu, their father.

"Separate your children," he commanded, "so that I can create the world and prevent the dark, watery wastes from returning."

Shu had to obey. He crawled between his son and daughter. Then he levered Nut upwards as if he were raising a tent of blue, and held Geb down firmly under his feet.

Geb struggled to free himself. His growls sent the first earthquakes shuddering through the land and he spewed out the first volcanoes in temper. His mother, Tefnut, rushed to calm him with her soothing breath of rain, and her tears fell on the earth and grew into sweet-smelling plants.

Shu lifted Nut his daughter even higher until she arched in a silent vault over Geb, with her toes poised on the eastern rim of the world and her outstretched fingertips on the western rim. Geb strained upwards in an attempt to reach out to her. But Shu kept him firmly in place.

As Geb lay gazing up at Nut, his outline turned into the craggy mountains and valleys of the earth's crust. And his mother's tears flowed into rivers and gathered in lakes around him.

Then Atum the creator took pity on Geb as he lay so still and separate staring up at Nut. Atum created thousands and thousands of stars and sprinkled them over the length of Nut's body.

"There, Geb! Now you can see Nut in the darkness."

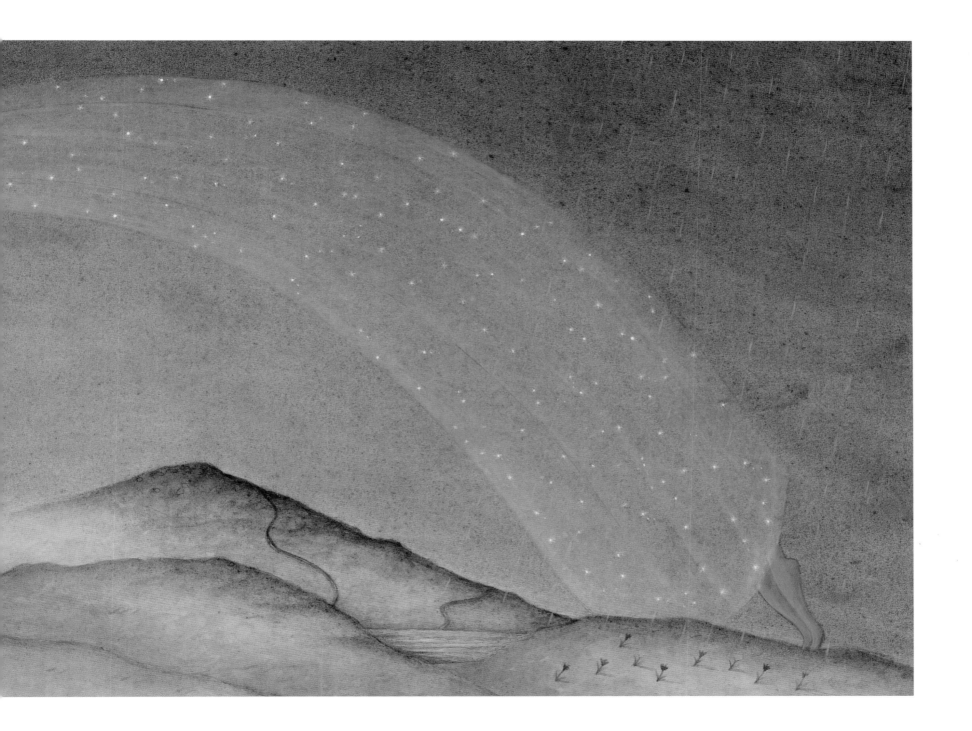

At last Atum had room to create whatever he desired. He scattered Nut's body with planets and a moon disc. Then he decorated Geb's dark skin with birds and beasts and plants.

He called out the names of gods to rule over them, and immediately the gods appeared ... gods of love, wisdom and justice.

Then Atum turned to Nut. "No child of yours shall spoil my creation or take my throne from me. I forbid you to give birth to a child on any day of the year!"

But something else happened. Thoth, the god of all wisdom, took pity on silent and beautiful Nut. He saw how lonely she was.

"You *shall* have children," he whispered. "I will find extra days in the year for you to have them."

So Thoth visited Khonsu, the god of the moon. He drew squares on a slate, and challenged Khonsu to a game of chequers played with light and dark moonstones.

Every time Thoth placed a dark
stone over one of Khonsu's light stones,
Khonsu had to give up some light.
Thoth managed to win five extra days
of light for Nut to give birth.

Osiris was born on the first day,

Horus on the second,

Seth on the third,

Isis on the fourth, and Nepthys on the fifth.

And since that time,
the moon has never been as
bright or as round as the sun.

After an eternity, Atum the creator grew old and tired. His bones turned to silver and his flesh to gold. He watched Nut's first-born son, Osiris, grow tall and strong, and his heart softened. "Osiris shall have my throne!" he announced. "I will retire to the heavens."

So Nut took Atum in her arms and lifted him up into the heavens.

　　Now at last Nut is content. She gathers the golden disc of Atum in the east each morning and guides his journey across the sky. Then she gently lowers him in the west each evening.

On some days she is crystal-clear aquamarine. On others, she is milky-white moonstone or opaque as turquoise.

Sometimes she has the lustre of opal, at other times the brilliance of sapphire. Occasionally she is the deep, dark blue of lapis lazuli. And always at night, she enfolds the dark onyx sky against her star-studded bosom.

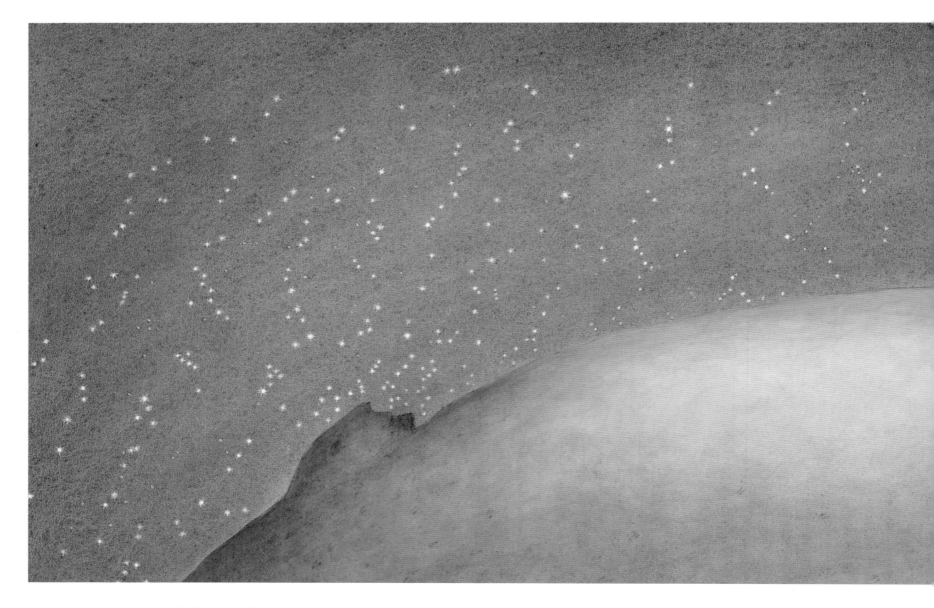

Now Geb lies silently gazing at Nut, enchanted by all her moods. Sometimes Shu's arms grow tired of holding Nut's body with its weight of stars. Then Nut leans down and tells secrets to her old love, Geb.

On these nights the stars seem especially bright and close to the earth,
and Nut's whispers float down softly as stardust.

MORE TITLES ILLUSTRATED BY JUDE DALY AND PUBLISHED BY FRANCES LINCOLN CHILDREN'S BOOKS

The Stone – A Persian Legend of the Magi
Dianne Hofmeyr

In the Ancient Persian town of Saveh, three astronomers are gazing up at the heavens when a star like no other appears, filling the sky with fiery light. Discovering in their ancient scrolls that it marks the birth of a remarkable baby, they set off to honour the child – bearing gold, myrrh and incense. But when they present their gifts, the child gives them in return a small sealed box, and the three men are mystified…
ISBN 978-0-7112-1320-3

To Every Thing There is a Season

The well-loved words of Ecclesiastes take on new life and meaning in the sun-baked rural setting of a South African homestead. Sowing, planting and reaping through the wet and dry seasons, going to market, day-to-day dealings with neighbours and acquaintances, love and hostility, the sadness of mourning and the joy of celebration with family and friends.
ISBN 978-1-84507-344-2

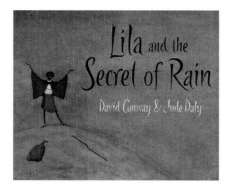

Lila and the Secret of Rain
David Conway

One night Lila overheard her mama talking about the well that had dried up and the crops that were failing. "Without water there can be no life," Lila heard her mama say. Lila wanted so much for the sun to stop shining and for the rain to come.
ISBN 978-1-84507-407-4 (HB)

Frances Lincoln titles are available from all good bookshops.
You can also buy books and find out more about your favourite titles,
authors and illustrators on our website: www.franceslincoln.com